WHAT BOOKS PRESS

AN IMPRINT OF

THE GLASS TABLE

COLLECTIVE

LOS ANGELES

FIGURES OF WOOD

FIGURES OF WOOD

MARÍA PÉREZ-TALAVERA

TRANSLATED BY PAUL FILEV

LOS ANGELES

Library of Congress Cataloging-in-Publication Data

Names: Pérez-Talavera, María, 1985- author. | Filev, Paul, translator.
Title: Figures of wood / Maria Pérez-Talavera ; translated by Paul Filev.
Other titles: Eran de madera. English
Description: Los Angeles : What Books Press, [2023] | Includes
    bibliographical references. | Summary: "Figures of Wood is a work of
    fiction that questions reality and sanity through the mind of L, a
    person confined to a sanatorium"-- Provided by publisher.
Identifiers: LCCN 2023024984 (print) | LCCN 2023024985 (ebook) | ISBN
    9798986625836 (paperback) | ISBN 9798986625898 (epub)
Subjects: LCGFT: Psychological fiction. | Diary fiction. | Novels.
Classification: LCC PQ8550.426.E77 E7313 2023 (print) | LCC PQ8550.426.E77
    (ebook) | DDC 863/.7--dc23/eng/20230523
LC record available at https://lccn.loc.gov/2023024984
LC ebook record available at https://lccn.loc.gov/2023024985

Cover art: Gronk, *Untitled*, 2022
Book design by ash good, www.ashgood.com

What Books Press
363 South Topanga Canyon Boulevard
Topanga, CA 90290

WHATBOOKSPRESS.COM

To Marcelo Sinán,
the boy who teaches me
how to
GROW

CONTENTS

the reporter's lead flies swiftly
over the notebook

It seems like Monday because yesterday felt more like a dull Sunday to me. It rained in the afternoon and they brought me a pastry and a cup of hot chocolate to my room. The woman with purple hair sat with me until I had finished the snack. Her eyes remind me of those physical maps that hang on classroom walls, fine veins streaking across the whites of her eyes like rivers. I ate and drank slowly, without talking or becoming distracted, savoring every bite and sip, licking my fingers and dabbing up all the crumbs off the plastic tray and then placing them on the tip of my tongue. Whenever I looked up, I met her watchful gaze.

Outside my room I hear the sounds announcing the start of the week: the footsteps scurrying up and down the hallway; the squeaking of laundry and cleaning cart wheels; buzzers, bells, and garbled announcements over the speaker; the receptionist's phone ringing a few feet away from my room (her desk faces my doorway); the dry cough of the police officer stationed by my door. On Monday mornings, the nurse on duty comes by my room to review my medications in my file, which hangs in a plastic holder on the door. He is young and muscular. His white teeth contrast with his skin color. His hair is short at the back and sides and long on top and he uses hair gel to keep it in place. He's always smiling and it really bugs me. I suspect he's making fun of me, that he gets a kick out of making me squirm, especially when he takes me out of my room against my will. The last time he took me to Dr. O'Malley's office, he whistled and hummed a tune all the way there, even when we were inside the small elevator. The lack of space in the elevator makes me uncomfortable. We stood so close to each other, I could smell his aftershave, and as he whistled, I could feel his breath as it exhaled, hitting my face with an intensity that changed with every note. It was disgusting. He asked me if I knew the tune. I shook my head. And frankly, I didn't care to know. We got out of the elevator and I was almost glad to be at the doctor's office, if not for the fact that I don't like being questioned by Dr. O'Malley. He repeats the same questions in every session, in a patronizing tone that gets on my nerves. I try to answer calmly and with composure, but sometimes it's just beyond me. That day, however, I managed to stay calm during the session and was even polite and friendly. I asked the doctor for a glass of water (I had woken up thirsty) and laughed at his joke about the big ugly birds. He makes the same joke every time to gauge my mood. The doctor stared at me throughout the session with an ambiguous look on his face—with an expression that could pass for either attentiveness or boredom—and he hardly blinked at all. At the end of the session, as I was leaving, out of the corner of my eye I saw him loosen the knot of his tie with one hand while hurriedly jotting down notes in the yellow folder with my name on it with his other hand. Anyway, I think the nurse's visit just confirms that today is Monday.

A few days ago, when Señorita Ritter came by, I had no idea what day of the week it was. That afternoon had the brightness of a Friday about it, but deep down, the hopelessness of a Wednesday. What's certain is that, as usual, Señorita Ritter had brought me a package wrapped in brown paper and tied with a string. She normally hands me the package as soon as she

arrives and I put it straight down on the nightstand with a show
of appreciation but also indifference. I don't want her to think that
the best part of her visit is her gift for me. I then give her my full
attention. We stare out into the garden, where others stroll along
the paved path or sit on the benches under the shade of the trees,
sheltering from the sun or maybe from themselves. She watches me
as I rearrange my wooden figures on the windowsill. The look on
her face tells me what she's thinking. We read for a while, with her
sitting in the armchair in the corner and me on the bed. Sharing
our silence is wonderful. Her visits always last the same length of
time and I know when they're over because she suddenly interrupts
what she's doing to glance at her wristwatch and pick up her bag.
From the doorway, I lock onto her cat eyes, magnified by the thick
lenses of her glasses. We take leave of each other with a gesture
of goodbye that is barely perceptible. I don't know when she'll
return. I just know that she will keep coming back. The dynamic
between us was different on her last visit. When she handed me
the package wrapped in brown paper, she urged me to open it. I
didn't know what to do, so I just took it and walked over to the
armchair in the corner. I sat down with my legs close together and
placed the package on my knees. I searched her face for further
instructions and again she motioned to me to unwrap it. I untied
the string and carefully peeled open the edges (I usually save the
paper from each of her packages). I was surprised to see a small
black leather notebook with rounded corners, an elastic strap, and
a ribbon bookmark. There was also a silver plated pen with which
I am now writing down these words. My first instinct was to look
out through the window in the door of my room. I thought the
pen might be one of those prohibited objects. But she placed her
hand reassuringly on my arm. The physical contact surprised me
more than the gift. I stood quite still, feeling the sensation of her
skin on mine. She said something and I had to ask her to repeat
it because I was so shocked by the sound of her voice that I didn't

pay attention to her words. The day after her visit—or perhaps a few days after, I'm not sure—I told the woman with purple hair I wanted to see the supervisor. That afternoon, the supervisor came to my room. When I showed him the pen and notebook and asked for permission to use them, I thought he would just grab them out of my hands and leave. He gave me a defiant look and then left the room. A short while later he came back to tell me that Dr. O'Malley had said it was okay for me to keep the pen and notebook. On the spectrum of positive emotions, I suppose I felt happy. It was as if a new dimension had opened up, as if thousands of opportunities were presenting themselves. I guess you could call that happiness. For several nights, I thought about what to write. I would stroke the cover of the notebook, leafing through the pages one by one, imagining them filled with interesting scrawls and impressive ideas. I agonized at the thought of messing up these pages with empty phrases and nonsense; or worse, that they would remain blank forever, waiting in vain for something wonderful to come out of me. Señorita Ritter had said to me, "Make good use of it," and now I have that weight on my shoulders. I cannot fail her. Today I woke up thinking it seemed like Monday, and Monday is a day for beginnings. When I have a clear head, I will jot down my thoughts. I will tell you everything that has so far filled our silences.

TUESDAY.

In my childhood, every day was the same. Mist would
hang in the morning air and the evening twilight would creep
in through the billowing muslin curtains in the living room.
At the end of the afternoon, Teresa would stoop down with
difficulty to pick up my toys, her knees cracking. I would
run around the room, buying myself some more time, until
eventually she cornered me and, one by one, pried open my
fingers to extricate the wooden figures from my sweaty palms.
I would not put up a fight. Regardless, she would put all the
figures back up on the high shelf, where they have sat arranged
in formation for more than eighty years, displaying the
imperfect splendor of a humble collection.

In this place of confinement, every day is the same.
Stuck here, now I just wander through the memories of my
childhood. I can picture all the wooden figures in detail and
have gradually called to mind the other things in the big house:
the books in the library, the silverware, the bottles of vinegary
wine from the cellar, the empty matchboxes, the lamps draped
with filmy cobwebs, the tablecloths, the mirrors, the portraits.
Like Camus's Meursault, I have dedicated myself to making a
mental inventory of the objects from what was my home and,
inevitably, to recalling the events that led to my being confined

to this room. It would be tedious for me to write down a list of all the things I can remember and perhaps even futile to relive what happened. If I end up making one, it will serve merely to outline the memories I conjure up, an attempt to condense the past, a dangerous game of recreating those bitter moments of my life before I came to this place. In no way am I seeking extenuating circumstances for my crime.

Here in my new quarters, I have almost the same provisions as in the big house: the occasional, usually dull visitor, food, a room of my own, and even a few books. The only irreplaceable things are my wooden figures from the living room.

When my grandfather was a young boy, he would sit next to his grandfather in the rocking chair on the balcony as the sun was going down, and together they would carve small pieces of wood with ivory-handled knives. The rocking motion helped to exert force on the piece of wood, while the late afternoon sun cast a soft orange glow over the old man's swift strokes and the child's clumsy cuts. Between them, they made a virtual army of small figures, reproducing, in a certain way, the people of their hometown, where my father was also born and where I now live and always have lived. Almost all the figures are in some sort of active pose, participating in various scenes of daily life: hammering, milking, raising hands in prayer, casting a fishing line, or serving tea. Many of them are holding an imaginary object. Accordingly, an assortment of miniature accessories such as a hammer, a cow with heavy udders, a bible, a fishing rod, a silver tray and tea set, and dozens of other curiosities can be found cluttered in a wood and ivory box together with the carving knives. Each tiny object fits perfectly in the appropriate figure's hands. There is, however, one exception to the figures in an active pose: a figure standing with his feet together and arms at his sides and his right hand, barely discernible, pointed like a blade just above his pants pocket. My guess is that this was one of my great-grandfather's late carvings, when his arthritic fingers no longer allowed him to sculpt on a miniature scale. Or perhaps one of my grandfather's early carvings, when he was still learning the craft. At any rate, it looked like a figure with no obvious trade. All the figures were oil-painted. Despite the passing of the years, the smell of the paint still lingered on the wood. In some cases, as with the blacksmith, there were places where the colors bled over the outlines. The dark pigment of his skin dripped down onto his shirt collar, over the side of the anvil, and completely camouflaged the mallet in his hand. On other figures, the dripping of paint was intentional, like the butcher, whose apron as well as his hands and face were spattered red. Curiously, none of the figures in the collection had a face.

When I was in elementary school, I was too short to reach the high shelf with the wooden figures and I would ask my mother or Teresa to take them down for me. They would give me a handful or two and sometimes the small box containing the clutter of miniature accessories. I would have to make do with examining just that random selection up close. As for the other figures, I had to content myself with observing them from a distance. I imagined the faces of each one, or rather substituted them for those of the neighbors, the servants, or the members of our family. The sensation of holding the wooden figures in my hands, of pressing my fingertips into the grooves and running them over the rough cuts, gave me a strange pleasure. Whenever a splinter broke off and embedded itself under my skin, it forged a connection with that character. Though they had no eloquent facial features, I could sense their moods, their expressions of joy and sorrow, their light and dark emotions.

On some afternoons, after I finished playing with them, I would hide a few of the figures in one of my socks, before Teresa came into the living room to put them back up on the high shelf and get me ready for dinner. Then when I went to bed that night, after my mother had tucked me in and left the room, I would enjoy their company. The moonlight—when there was a moon—would cast a soothing blue glow over us. Other times, a flashlight served as sunlight in the darkness. The figures spoke to me without mouths, heard me without ears. The night I abducted the ringmaster (with a top hat perched above a mane of wild hair), Father came home from one of his trips. He crept quietly into my room, thinking I was asleep. The sheet was pulled up over my head. He pulled it down to allow me to breathe better and caught me red-handed playing with the wooden figure. He snatched it out of my hand and gave me a stern look. "Don't ever do that again. The figures must stay on the shelf in the living room. They mustn't get lost." Then he added—more to himself than to me—that there used to be a hundred and twenty figures and only a hundred and nine were left. "You haven't thrown any away, have you?" I just shook my head. It's true I sometimes secretly took some of them to spend the night away from the shelf, but I always brought them back to the living room the following afternoon for Teresa to return them to their place. Father kissed my forehead and then left the room. The sound of his footsteps faded down the stairs.

That's how I found out that eleven figures were missing. For years, I have racked my brain trying to imagine who those characters could be. While walking down the street or reading the newspaper or browsing through the archives in the library, I would assign random faces to the missing figures. I noticed there was no librarian among the collection (perhaps there were no libraries in the town when my grandfather was small, just as there were no cars, which explains why there was no mechanic in the collection either). That's when I decided to expand the collection by adding some of my own creations. The first piece I attempted—and haven't yet finished—is that of a librarian.

*Patriarchs sit at supper with sons
and grandsons and great grandsons
around them,*

I wish I had some of my books here with me, but given the circumstances in which I was brought to this residence, I had no time to pack any. All I have are the wooden figures that were in my pockets at the time, nothing more. Fortunately, Señorita Ritter supplies me with books. I devoured the first few she gave me, but I've since learned to enjoy them slowly in order to shorten the wait time between one book and another. Besides, I tend to fall asleep after reading only a few pages.

One day shortly after I arrived here, I was being led back to my room after a session with Dr. O'Malley when I passed by what looked like a recreation room. I spotted some playing cards, checkers and chess sets, and books on a shelf at the back of the room. I asked the nurse if we could stop for a moment before going back to the room. To my surprise, he actually agreed, but not before tightening his grip on my arm even more. I looked at the selection of books under the watchful eye of my guard. I was a little disappointed to find there were only romance novels, Sunday magazines, and some children's books (which I thought quite strange, because this place isn't a children's or youth center, plus I know that I'm the youngest one here). The nurse picked up a reading primer and said sarcastically, "Do you want this one? It's time to go." Then he led me by the arm back to my room.

At home, Father has a library stocked with dusty classics. I've read most of them more than once, with the exception of the encyclopedias, the cookbooks, and books in Latin or French. By the time I was twelve and in middle school, I was taller and could reach the high shelf with the wooden figures on my own and do what I wanted with them. I could also apply for a library card at the town library, which is something I did right away.

The library is housed in the former town hall. Though small and old, the building has a lot of character. Its stone wall façade is adorned with wooden beams and large windows on either side. The front porch columns and sides of the building are covered in moss and colorful wildflowers. This patchwork of elements gives it a quaint feel that is out of tune with the surrounding buildings. Its exterior shape looks like a classic child's drawing of a house: an isosceles triangle over a rectangle. At night, the front is lit up by dim yellow bulbs hidden in the eaves, and—thanks to the lamps on the library study tables—from the outside one can admire the stillness and silence of the interior.

It became part of my routine to stop by the library after school. I could spend hours in that magnificent room filled with books and papers, reading thrillers, Gothic literature, and crime and horror fiction. I sometimes read other things too. But I was always drawn back to the works of Poe, Chandler, Hammett, Doyle . . .

Later on, I became obsessed with the archives section of the library, poring over the historical and genealogical records of the area. I looked through the old dusty albums filled with grainy photographs in sepia tones, gazing at the faces and imagining them in possession of the souls of the wooden figures from my collection. I began researching things about the local

area, the social and political events of my great-grandfather's and
my grandfather's era, because it was around that time that they
began carving the collection. I was eager to make a connection
between the actual people and the carved figures left behind as
a legacy by my ancestors. I felt—and still feel—a huge need to
know every last detail of their existence. I started with my own
family, transcribing their records into a notebook. One day when
Father was having dinner at home, I pulled out a few sheets from
my pocket and excitedly began telling him what I'd learned.
I told him that we were related to several families in the area,
mentioning some long funny names and how many times his
first name had been passed down from generation to generation.
I glanced up every so often to see my father's reactions, but he
just kept chewing his food and taking small sips from his glass of
wine. He didn't seem to be as amazed or amused as I was. Then
my mother took the papers from my hand and told me to go to
my room and get ready for bed. I hadn't even eaten and went to
bed without dinner. The next day I continued looking into family
trees, but those of other families in our town. Before long, I could
rattle off the names of the ancestors and the blood and marital
relatives of the neighbors from our block.

It was at the town library where I met Señorita Ritter,
the librarian. She was a woman in her thirties and always had
a freshly showered look about her, smelling of *Jean Naté* soap
and talcum powder. She was new to me and I knew nothing
about her. When our eyes met for the first time, her gaze pierced
right through me, just like one of the many splinters embedded
deep under my skin. I have to say that from that moment on
an inexplicable connection was forged between us: she was a
mystery to me, but somehow, we could read each other perfectly.
It sounds clichéd—and I hate clichés—but it was as if we had
known each other all our lives.

From the outset, she knew which books to recommend to me. She would take me by the hand and lead me either to a wide bookcase filled with new titles, a section with a small collection of literary treasures, or one with a handful of rare books. Her thin, wiry fingers fit perfectly in my hand. On some afternoons, as soon as I entered the library, she would hand me a book and greet me with a wink of her cat-shaped eye. Magnified by her glasses, her eyes held the promise of one who can take you to other worlds with a single gesture.

Thanks to Señorita Ritter, I delved into the world of poetry. It had never caught my attention before. We had read some poems in school, but nothing that ever grabbed me. The complexity of the poems and their strictly metered and rhymed forms were a source of great consternation to me: should I be moved by the poem's meaning or take delight in its sound? In time, I came to understand that poetry is the mathematics of language. The science of the word. The essentiality of experience. A poem's beauty is reflected in the musicality of its verses and in its vital silences. Feelings are transposed onto the page, and all boundaries—physical, mental, spiritual—are blurred. Apotheosis is its conduit; the sublime, its goal. Poetry is the mystery of simplicity.

I read whatever I could get my hands on, including what little I found of Pessoa and his heteronyms. I was captivated by his writing. You could say I read Whitman to death, but the truth is I never got tired of rereading him. *Leaves of Grass* was like a bible to me, a book to decipher. Whitman's free verse poems liberated me from the constraints of meter and rhyme, from the imposition of archaic forms. In them I found encrypted messages about my own existence, a Song to myself. To read Whitman was to animate my collection of wooden figures:

The butcher-boy puts off his killing-clothes, or sharpens his knife at
    the stall in the market,
I loiter enjoying his repartee and his shuffle and breakdown.

Blacksmiths with grimed and hairy chests environ the anvil,
Each has his main-sledge . . . they are all out . . . there is a great
    heat in the fire.

From the cinder-strewed threshold I follow their movements,
The lithe sheer of their waists plays even with their massive arms,
Overhand the hammers roll—overhand so slow—overhand so sure,
They do not hasten, each man hits in his place.

Large signs next to the wall clocks in the library
demanded "Silence." Señorita Ritter had a mouth, but didn't
speak to me; she had ears, but didn't seem to hear. I sat at the
study table, and there, under the soothing light of the banker's
lamp, I read the dark books that illuminated my world—the real
world, the one worth living in. In this way, the pages of the books
I read and the blank pages of my notebook became sacred portals
through which my life made sense. I began to compose my own
verses, to write my own stories, to develop characters that were
almost always physically based on the wooden figures in my
collection. To create this new dimension.

It's the start of the weekend, and with it comes the hope
of receiving, coming across, or at the very least, of remembering a
good book.

Mutis.

From the orbit of your eye breaks forth

a silent dawn

a flickering firefly

pulsing with light.

My chest is a hollow

that in its eternal night

quietly awaits

your flame.

L.

the gatekeeper marks who pass,

SATURDAY.

Saturdays are horrible. Even before the sun has risen, I can already hear the other residents on the floor getting ready for the usual hustle and bustle of the weekend. The young guy in the room next to mine calls out for someone named Gisela. But whoever she is, she never appears. The only person who looks in at his door is the floor supervisor. After the supervisor's three unsuccessful attempts to calm him down, two nurses rush in to control the situation. By then it's time for me to get up.

Without a word of greeting, the woman with purple hair enters my room busily and speaks to me as if we were in mid-conversation. I can tell what she's thinking just by looking at her face. She has spent so many nights on the armchair in my room or on the other side of the wall—inducing, monitoring, and interrupting my sleep—that she's like an appendage, a recurrent presence in my unremarkable and indistinct days. In this place our lives are a continuous thread, an endless hallway, an eternal night where greetings—"hello," "good morning," "goodbye," and "see you tomorrow"—are meaningless. We have been thrown into a mundane coexistence where politeness is not required.

While I'm taking my shower, I hear the sound of muffled crying coming from the adjoining shower stall. I try not to guess which of my neighbors it is by concentrating on how hungry I am. I suppose Saturday breakfast is my favorite— at least we're given options—although I hate it that all I can manage are two or three bites before I lose my appetite. I don't mind leaving behind a half-eaten piece of fruit or pancake on my plate, but the caregivers seem to get annoyed if I don't eat everything I'm served and that sometimes creates problems for me. So occasionally, and if I'm in the mood, I finish all my food in order to avoid trouble, especially if I want (or rather need) to go outside.

Saturdays are visitors' days and we're allowed to stroll through the garden. There are even those who attend yoga classes in the dining room or meditation classes in the recreation room or play ball on the courts. Dr. O'Malley is always happy when he finds out I went for a walk in the fresh air or did some physical exercise. "It will help you," he says. The truth is I find that hard to believe. Anyway, when I don't have anything to read, I like to go outside for a walk in the hope of finding a book lying around. I rarely succeed, but today I'm feeling lucky.

It's a hot and humid day and the heat outside is brutal. I have two minders, one on either side of me. They chat to each other, ignoring me while keeping an eye on me at the same time, and they don't hesitate to invade my body space. One talks about how hard it has been having a fourth child. The other responds with things that seem to have nothing to do with what the first one said and mentions God a lot. There are more people out than usual, and in contrast to the solitude and monotony of my days, I am glad to be out in the crowded gardens. More often than not, some of the residents are carrying books, given to them by their relatives. But they're incapable of reading. I wonder if today I will come across one of them.

There's a low area in the garden that's been flooded by
rain. As we descend the slope, the puddle comes into view as
a blot on an otherwise dull landscape. I bend down to pick up
some stones from the ground. The minders suddenly stop their
conversation. I sense their alarm. I toss a pebble into the puddle
to prove my innocent intention: throwing stones in the water.
When the pebble hits the puddle, it splashes muddy water
onto the white pants of one of the minders. Now it's me who is
alarmed. Will he take this as an act of aggression? The minder
reads and understands my gesture. He shoots an annoyed
look at the offending stain on his pants and puts an end to
the scene by saying: "Let's go back to the path. The garden
is waterlogged." Unfortunately, my excursion is short-lived
because of my stupidity.

As we join the others on the path, the bunch of people
around me becomes more noticeable. This strange tribe, of which
I am now a part, to which I now belong. I wonder if I look as
bizarre as them or even worse. On one side of the pathway is
a sitting area with a pergola covered with transparent panels.
A gnarled tree with twisted branches rears above it. Plump
raindrops thump against the roof. Creepers with masses of yellow
flowers climb up around the green steel posts of the pergola. Tiny
butterflies flutter past, unnoticed by the passersby, even when
they land on their shoulders, their hair, or their foreheads. The
minders cut through the pergola area. I have a strong sensation
of crossing a threshold. The people scattered about are locked
in a bizarre collective dance without realizing it, moving to the
rhythm of the sounds inside the pergola area. Near the exit, a
woman cackles shrilly while the man next to her drones on. A
long strand of drool hangs from his lower lip. I spot the object
I've been looking for, tucked under the man's right armpit. I make
a beeline for it. The minders react immediately and wordlessly.

"What's the book?"

The man mutters something unintelligible, though I sense it's not in answer to my question.

"Will you lend me your book?" I say, holding out my hand to the man. The minders stare at me hesitantly.

The man continues mumbling. I take a step forward. I walk right up to him. My fingertips brush the spine of the book when one of the minders pushes my hand away. This sudden reflex action makes the man finally look up at me.

Hazy orange clouds in the sky. The smell of pine in the air. A squall indicates a coming storm. A calloused hand with grimy fingernails places the prize in my grasping hand.

With the book in my possession, I am at the mercy of the minders. They march me up the stone path once again to the seclusion of my room with the familiar stench of mothballs, a smell I know so well. From the other side of the wall—just a few steps away from me—a watchful gaze peers in through the hinges of the door.

*The duck-shooter walks by silent
and cautious stretches,*

SUNDAY.

In my frequent visits to the library, I got to know others
like me who felt at home among the bookshelves and even in the
silence. I have no friends other than my wooden figures, but I
don't have any problems striking up a conversation with others to
talk about books. One Saturday morning, an old woman who was
reading next to me tried to engage me in a conversation. She was
curious about the book I was reading, or to be more precise, she
was shocked by it (a book by D. H. Lawrence, I don't remember
which one). The fact is that after a heated discussion about
the book's, or rather, the author's alleged indecency—alleged
by her of course—we ended up having a coffee together at the
corner store, where we talked about the various classics we had
read. Another person I met in the library was Mihail, a kid who
looked a lot like Martin Luther and who, like him, had the habit
of wearing a black cap. He was an avid comic book collector.
Whenever we ran into each other in the library, he would try to
convince me to start my own collection. The comics that reached
our town were old editions, so Mihail would often travel to the
capital or other neighboring cities in order to get his hands on
the most recent editions. What struck me about his collection
of comic books was that many of them were still unread. He'd
never even so much as flicked through them. He kept them in
protective plastic sleeves so as not to damage them. This made

no sense to me at all. Why would you buy a book you had no intention of reading?

But it was probably Don Gastón, the pharmacist, who, together with me, was the most regular visitor to the library. I remember him invariably sitting at one of the front tables, closest to the desk where Señorita Ritter worked. He usually read the periodicals and occasionally flicked through pharmaceutical guidebooks or weighty tomes on various topics. He had a thin white mustache and small dark and bright eyes that darted around restlessly, following the movements around him. His gray face—the same color as his thinning hair—was hidden behind the daily newspaper. Don Gastón was a mouse of human proportions.

We knew each other only by sight. We would pass each other without greeting, but at the same time we would silently acknowledge our mutual presence, which revolved around the same sun. That is until one day we met by chance at a book flea market in the park, where people came to buy and sell or swap their old books. I couldn't sell or swap any of Father's books, but I came with the pocket money I had saved up to buy whatever I wanted. Some vendors had spread their books on the ground under the shade of the trees while others had brought their own tables on which to display them. People strolled from one vendor to another in search of their next read. To my surprise, I saw Don Gastón, dressed in his usual attire of black trousers and white shirt, standing beside his own stall. It was a hot morning. At first glance, the selection he had on display looked quite interesting. There were books on psychology, medicine, and a wide range of good literature, including some recent releases that weren't available at the town library. I stopped in front of his stall and we exchanged greetings with each other for the first time. I nodded to him and, before I could look down at the books, he held out his hand for me to shake. "I'm Gastón. What's your name?" We introduced ourselves stiffly and then I immediately began scouring the selection of books: Camus; a first edition of Kafka in German; Oscar Wilde; a variety of Russian writers—Chekhov, Tolstoy, Dostoyevsky, Nabokov, Belyaev; a rare volume of poetry by Faulkner (I didn't know he was a poet); and several women writers, some of whom he recommended: Virginia Woolf, Simone de Beauvoir, and a couple of Russian women poets whose names I don't recall. I confessed that I hadn't read many books written by women and he urged me to start doing so. In fact, he pressed a copy of *The Second Sex* into my hands, along with an edition of *Epoch Magazine* from 1966, which included the short story "Where Are You Going, Where Have You Been?" by Joyce Carol Oates. He described her as a rising literary star and said he thought I might enjoy her story (which seemed strange to me, seeing as how he had no way of knowing my tastes).

From that day on, whenever we saw each other in the library, we would exchange greetings in an almost friendly manner. And if we bumped into each other at the café, we would swap notes on what books we had been reading. I once asked him why he never read works of literature in the library. "I do my reading for pleasure at home. In the library, I'm taken up with other concerns." That made sense.

Twice a month, Don Gastón would pass by our house on his way to work at the pharmacy and leave me a brown paper package tied with string. Sometimes he would hand the package directly to my mother or else he would just drop it into our mailbox and then Teresa would give it to me later on at dinnertime. The packages contained all kinds of books, usually ones not found on the library's shelves. The

accompanying note in his scrawl always read the same:
"For young L. Enjoy the books."

At first the packages were modest, containing only one or two books. Whenever I received one, I would go up to him in the library and discreetly thank him. He would peer over the top of his newspaper at me and just nod his head. Later the packages became more extravagant, and if I'm not mistaken, I would say more costly as well. Sometimes they contained three or four books—always new ones—including limited editions, beautiful hardcovers, and the latest issues of literary magazines. Don Gastón noticed I would spend hours in the archive section of the library. I know this because he always made sure to give me a slight nod in greeting through the fish tank, which I sat behind in seclusion with the old and delicate books. That is how he found out about my interest in genealogy. Right after that, I received a brown paper package, a first edition of *One Hundred Years of Solitude*, published ten years earlier by Editorial Sudamericana. I enjoyed the task of plotting the Buendía family tree as much or even more than the book itself.

I had no idea why this man who I barely knew insisted on giving me such thoughtful gifts. At first I welcomed them. But after a while the situation began to bother me. In some way, I felt as if I owed him something in exchange for his generosity. For her part, Mother soon noticed that what seemed an occasional gesture had turned into something habitual.

"The pharmacist has given you several books."

I nodded.

"Why does he give them to you?"

"I don't know."

"Did you ask for them?"

"Of course not, Mamá."

"Then, why does he bring them to the house?"

"I guess he likes me. Or he likes the fact that I read."

My mother looked into my eyes for a few seconds, trying to work out what I was thinking. Then she gave a snort accompanied by a little smirk, a gesture she usually makes when internalizing what I say. Even so, her mind still wanders down unfathomable paths.

The young fellow drives the express-wagon
. . . I love him though I do not know him;

That night, the temperature had dropped more than usual. Luckily, I had packed a sweater in my backpack, along with a few other provisions: a cheese sandwich, an apple, and a thermos of tea. I had a pair of binoculars with me too. I found them one afternoon a few months ago while looking for something or other in a dresser drawer. Besides the binoculars, there were also a number of other objects in the drawer. They looked as if they had been stashed away in there for years and they drew my attention for the rest of the afternoon: a bunch of medals, badges, and photographs of my father dressed in military uniform. There's no denying it, he looked young and strong, and extremely handsome too. His face bore a serious expression, with no hint of joy on it, as if a part of his role was to be miserable. One photograph showed a group of men in fatigues. But it wasn't the uniform that made them all look alike; it was the bitterness written on their faces.

That's how I found out that my father had served in the army in the past. It broke my heart and explained the unbridgeable distance between us. What else has my father done that I don't know about? Who is that taciturn man who sits down to dinner at our table, sleeps in the same bed as my mother, and kisses my forehead in the morning before going off again? Sometimes he seems like a complete stranger to me who only occasionally spends the night at our home and I have to try to fill in the blank spaces of his life. What was his childhood like? Which soccer team does he follow? Why did he never carve figures with my grandfather?

My grandfather and I enjoyed strolling together around the property. We took long leisurely walks along a maze of tracks, which seemed to act as a backdrop to the anecdotes he related. I would listen to him, entranced by his frail voice, by the enchanting landscape, and by the smell of the grass—green or dried—that we trampled over with our rubber boots. Never once during our many strolls together did Grandfather talk about Father. And something inside me told me it was better not to ask him any questions. Yet Father's presence was often implicit in some of Grandfather's stories, discernable in the tone of a throwaway remark or in the momentary heaviness of his eyelids. Grandfather would always carry a stick during our walks, which he pulled from one of the bushes around the house, to drive away insects or scare off wild animals. If after a longer silence than usual he waved the stick over his head, it gave me the impression he was trying to chase away bad memories. His memories were distant and yet quite vivid. However, if I asked him what he'd had for breakfast that morning, he couldn't tell me. He was like someone from a time machine, and this fascinated me, especially when he told me about how the collection of wooden figures came to be made. Everything I know about the figures, including the management and care of the collection, I learned from him: from how to hold the knife, to the basic carving techniques and tips for painting and finishing them. He showed me the willows where the wood for the figures originally came from, how to choose the best stump, and how to prime the wood before painting it. He introduced me to the wonderful world of oil paints. He taught me how to prepare and bottle them in clear or amber jars and then label them with a color code. He instructed me on how to use a paintbrush, a gouge, a plane, sandpaper, a spatula, and other workshop tools.

Grandfather built the shed behind the house to use as a workshop. It was there where he created the wooden figures and their accessories made of various other materials: copper, silver, aluminum, steel, plastic, and other metals. If he didn't know how to work with a particular material, he would spend hours reading up on it in old pamphlets and books, or he would pay a visit to the workshops of the town carpenters, blacksmiths, cabinetmakers, and sculptors in order to learn from them, or else he would invite resourceful makers into his own workshop to help him materialize his miniature creations.

I miss Grandfather. I miss his reliable presence, his gentle gaze, and his shaggy gray beard. That stubborn beard, which he stroked gently, as if coaxing out the memories that seemed to be hidden within its tangles.

I also have a vivid memory of his bushy eyebrows, arching over the magnifying glass while his gnarled but precise fingers worked on carving miniature bouquets of flowers, cutlery sets, tools, puppies, or babies.

That night, when I brought the binoculars up to my eyes, for a moment I felt like him.

I chose this exact spot after staking out the block for several days. I had walked up and down the street after school each day, inspecting every corner near the library, looking for the best vantage point. I checked the light at different times of

the day to determine which corner best allowed me to watch
the comings and goings at the library without being seen. First
I considered taking up position in the small square diagonally
opposite the library on the other side of the street, but there were
no sculptures or shrubs to hide behind and I could easily be seen
from the library window.

Then I thought about planting myself in front of the row
of shops that extended out from one side of the small square.
But I would need a ready excuse for why I was hanging around
outside the shops that long. My espionage work would extend
beyond their closing time and it would look suspicious for me to
be just loitering on the sidewalk. After that I thought of going to
the churchyard like any other parishioner. But as the church was
on the same side of the street as the library, my target would not
be visible. I also tried the vantage point from the corner cafe, but
all I could see from there was just one side of the library building,
and not the main entrance.

All the other places around the library are private
residences. It's an old, quiet neighborhood made up of middle-
class families. The houses all look the same: single-story
structures with a spacious front yard, once decorated with
ornamental shrubs that today look like twisted green monsters.
I walked around the houses nearest to the library in search of
a possible hideout. They looked abandoned to me, as if the
owners had gone off to live somewhere else and left them in the
care of a gardener to look after the lawns and make sure they
weren't overrun by weeds. The old architecture, the dull colors,
and the peeling paint projected a palpable sense of neglect. But
the houses weren't empty. And while I scouted around for a
good hiding spot, I observed the daily activities of the families
who lived in them: mothers feeding their babies; children

running around the garden or riding their bicycles in the street; fathers racing out the front door, hurrying back to work after having lunch at home; door-to-door vendors selling cookware sets and membership subscriptions.

Number 16 looked the worst. The front porch was strewn with envelopes, brochures, and flyers. The front door slot was jammed full of them too. I approached discreetly to study the mess and saw that the mail was from long ago. The yellowed envelopes bore the scars of the weather's extremes. I didn't need to look in through the window to know the place was abandoned. It was obvious. I walked around the front yard. The library was visible from any vantage point. And the unpruned monsters would lend me their shadows.

Just as a precaution, I decided to inspect the back of the property. I jumped over the little gate to the side of the garage and explored the much smaller backyard. I tried to open the sliding door and the side door of the terrace, but they were both locked. I looked around under the mat and in the flowerpots for a key but without success. In the end, I decided that I would hide in the front yard. I would have to come after dark, so none of the neighbors would see me. And I would have to bring the binoculars with me. Even though there was a direct and unobstructed view of the library from the front yard, there was a considerable distance between the two places, further complicated by the darkness.

The long-planned day arrived at last. I would follow Señorita Ritter to her house and find out where she lived. My reason for wanting to know this? None in particular. Just to know more about her. After all, you can't just go up to a stranger and ask them where they live without seeming suspicious or like a stalker.

I imagined her living in a small building, three or four
stories high, with a narrow balcony overlooking the main street.
Perhaps one of those buildings with shops on the ground floor (a
quiet laundromat that lulls her to sleep at night with its humming
sounds; a French bakery that sells the most delicious Proustian
madeleines; a lottery vendor that endows her with luck every
morning). It would be a one-room apartment, with a small living/
dining area filled with bookshelves. The kitchen would be very
small and equipped with fine china and a coffee set with silver
floral trim. The air would be filled with the smell of basil on the
windowsills. Next to the entrance would be a coat rack, on which
a felt hat, her leather bag, an umbrella, and her red and black
plaid coat would be hanging. The same coat she is wearing now as
she comes out of the library.

From my hiding place behind the bushes, I snatch up
my binoculars and follow her movements. She walks down the
steps of the main entrance with the languid ease of someone who
has no one at home waiting for her with dinner and wine and
the desire to cozy up with her on the sofa or in bed. When she
reaches the sidewalk, she looks both ways as if she's about to cross
the street. Then she turns back to look at the library. From the
movement of her head, it appears as if she is giving someone a
sign before she walks off to the right.

I get up and quickly sling my backpack over my shoulder.
I prepare to follow her, close at her heels, from the other side of
the street, blending into the shadows, mimicking the branches
swaying in the wind. Just before I reach the corner, I notice
another person walking down the same sidewalk as my target.
I stop for a moment and hide behind a tree. I reach for the
binoculars to get a good look at him. I don't recognize this
individual, but a hunch tells me to act with caution. I walk off

quickly to get ahead of him—staying on the other side of the street—to get a look at his face head-on. Señorita Ritter is already a block ahead of us. I can still see her plaid coat in the distance. Just as I turn to look at the man, a streetlamp lights him up like an apparition. And from where I'm standing, I immediately recognize those small dark and bright eyes, restlessly following the steady click-clack of the woman's heels.

The youth lies awake in the cedar-roofed garret and harks to the musical rain,

During the winter, hardly anyone came to the library. I took advantage of the peace and quiet, the feeling of being alone, and the pitter-patter of the rain to read poetry. Settled comfortably in my usual chair—a wing chair, from where I could see the entrance and the whole floor—every now and then I would glance up to see where Señorita Ritter was. She would be either behind the green-lit counter, scurrying between the shelves with an armful of books, or else out of sight somewhere. It was one of those wet winter days, and although it was late afternoon, the rain continued to fall. The view from the windows was obscured by a heavy curtain of rain and a thunderstorm was threatening. There were only a few captive readers inside, waiting out the downpour, among them Don Gastón. The library had stayed open past closing time. Don Gastón paced through the aisles, checking the shelves, compulsively looking at his watch, and serving himself one cup of coffee after another from the vending machine. He sat down next to me and just like that, interrupted my reading.

"Do you like poetry?"

"I quite like it."

". . . I saw what you were reading last week."

"Oh, yes. Señorita Ritter recommended it to me."

"I don't think it's a matter of quite liking it; I think you must benefit from it."

I didn't know what to say to him. I think he noticed the perplexed look on my face because he added:

"What I mean is, you would benefit more from the books that I have been sending you than what you're reading now."

"Thank you for the books you sent me. I've read them all."

"Good. I'll send you some new ones. Poetry's not for a boy like you."

As he got up to continue his tour around the library or to leave, I instinctively blurted out:

"Don't bother, Don Gastón."

"Pardon?"

"You needn't send me any more books. I can't keep accepting them."

With a confused but dignified expression on his face, he made a subtle bow and then took his leave without saying a word. A few weeks later I began attending high school. This brought about a change in my schedule, which meant I could no longer go to the library at the same time I used to and so I saw less and less of Don Gastón. This ultimately contributed to our estrangement from one another.

*The groups of newly-come immigrants
cover the wharf or levee,*

I have thought long and hard about how I should start this letter, because, although I know what I want to say to you, I'm not sure how to address you. The normal thing would be to begin the salutation with the conventional "Dear Señorita Ritter." In this case, however, the normal thing would not be right. I don't know why people insist on addressing someone they don't know or someone they just have a formal business relationship with as "Dear." But what seems normal to everyone, Señorita Ritter, is not always appropriate.

And yes I do know you. Well enough, at least, so that if we run into each other at the market we recognize each other right away and we greet each other warmly. You know my literary tastes—a very personal thing in my opinion. I know the clothes you wear and the type of perfume you put on every day. You know my daily schedule better than my own father does, as well as the personal information on my library card: my full name, address, date of birth, telephone number, and ID number. I have to say, you're ahead of the game here, as it wasn't until just recently that I was able to collect some of this information about you. I found out your full name from the town gazette that lists all government employees' names, job titles, and salaries. From there I just had to look up "Helen Ritter" in the phone book in order to get your phone number and address, which, by the way, is out of date, and it meant that I had to follow you home one day to find out your real home address. Forgive me in advance for my impudence. You have to understand that I don't like being at a disadvantage with respect to our relationship. I got your date of birth from the library's yearbook. As for your ID number, that's the least of my worries. I've already figured out a way of getting it. I love the fact that you're a mystery that I'm able to solve.

No, Señorita Ritter, a hackneyed "Dear" would not do us justice. All this mutual information known to both of us should make us intimate acquaintances, especially since the day when I followed you home. As you well know, I wasn't the only one who followed you home that day. I confess I was very surprised to see Don Gastón had done the same thing. Technically speaking, my knowing about your private life makes us intimate . . . friends? However, I have trouble accepting the fact that what we have between us should be considered as mere friendship. Although in reality, true friendship supposes a degree of mutual loyalty and trust. But this is something that may not exist between us yet, especially after the events that happened the day I followed you home. We might instead consider ourselves "silent confidants."

On the other hand, I can't help wondering what type of relationship you have with Don Gastón Heredia, the town pharmacist, married to Doña Mirna Estrada, granddaughter of a former mayor. Theirs is a sad, barren, and loveless marriage. Did you know that Don Gastón is also distantly related to his wife? Perhaps you didn't know this. I hope knowing this about him doesn't in the same way make me a close friend of his too, because the mere thought of this is absurd and makes me sick to the stomach.

As you can see, Señorita Ritter, there is sufficient reason for me to start this letter with something more forthright than a trite "Dear." Should I call you "my darling" or perhaps "my beloved?" It would be presumptuous of me to begin this letter with a brazen "My Beloved Señorita Ritter." Above all, it would be sappy and just plain silly. It would imply that the woman I love is sleeping with another man, and that wouldn't be right. Forgive me for passing judgement on you and making assumptions about you, but I have gone over the facts in my head repeatedly and I always come to the same conclusion: you are sleeping with Don Gastón.

That night, after following you home fourteen blocks, I stood behind a small tree on the sidewalk opposite and watched as you climbed the steps to the front door of a narrow two-story house with the number 7, sandwiched between two others that looked exactly like it. The porch was dark and run down. I saw you turn the key—which you fished out of your coat pocket—and go in, without turning on the porch light or the lights inside. Seven minutes later, Don Gastón entered your home. I was startled at first, and the worst thoughts crossed my mind: he's a stalker and he's caught her off guard and wants to hurt her. I have to rescue her! I sped across the street, breathing heavily, prepared to confront this low-life rodent to defend you. But just as I was about to climb the steps, the light in the front part of the house came on. I ducked behind the bushes and peered over them. Through the frosted glass window, I could see your silhouettes level with each other, rocking back and forth gently, without agitation or surprise. That image, together with the fact that Don Gastón did not have to pick the lock, confirmed to me that this rendezvous had to have been planned, desired, and agreed upon by both of you. I stayed crouched in the bushes and watched the both of you for the next twenty-nine minutes. I saw you both sipping from wine glasses (with red wine I imagine) and then sitting down at a table with the silhouette of a large vase in the center of it (with what looked like lilies in it). Don Gastón's shadow slinked over to your side of the table, positioning itself behind your shadow. Your shadow appeared to pace quickly away, as if fleeing from his.

A theatrical ballet, a slow and dramatic courtship. You left the room first, and he followed; but not before he turned off the light. And just as he did that, a dim yellow light appeared in the upper window. Your bedroom must be upstairs. It's the standard layout for this type of house, or am I mistaken Señorita Ritter? I had to climb up the fence—and in doing so my left elbow got caught on a protruding nail—to be able to see what was happening in the room. But it was all in vain. The binoculars were of no use to me either as, with a single tug, Don Gastón pulled down the curtain, leaving me in the dark, enveloped by the night fog.

I won't call you "my beloved." I won't call you "dear." I won't even call you by your name, Helen, which I like so much. You have a beautiful name, Helen, not to mention the beauty of Helen of Troy. I could have started this letter with "My darling Helen" if I wanted to. But that memory of Don Gastón's hand pulling down the curtain, plunging me into the fog, would just break my heart again. And I would no longer adore you. So from now on and forever more, I have decided I will just call you "Señorita Ritter"—"My Señorita Ritter"—with the respect and forgiveness you deserve. Exactly one hour had gone by since your rendezvous with Don Gastón began when he came out the front door. He stopped and looked around and then walked off in the same direction he had come from with a certain air of triumph, noticeable in the way he swaggered off.

Since that day, Señorita Ritter, my life has been bleak. My old refuge, the library, has remained out of my physical and emotional reach. It's not only the fact that I have begun attending high school— which is located on the opposite side of town—it's also that memory that keeps haunting me that has kept me away from there. Although, I have to confess, Señorita Ritter, you are on my mind every day, floating intact in a protective bubble, like a piece of fine china, or better yet, like a carved wooden figure.

On my way home after school, I pick up flat stones from the ground. When I pass by the lake, I stop to throw them in the water and watch them skip across the surface. When they plunk to the bottom, a wave of despair washes over me. It starts in the pit of my stomach and then fills my chest, resembling the unmistakable silhouette of a mushroom cloud, lodged in my chest, in my core, in my being. I look at the strangers, immigrants, scattered around the shore. They stare wistfully at the lake, with the characteristic pain of missing a loved one. I am just one more stranger, immigrant, among them, lost and pining for someone, making room for this new landscape in my all-consuming longing. Then the fog that envelops everything, that mists my vision and freezes my bones, once again settles over the lake. The pier disappears, and I am compelled to head home. There I submerge myself in my books, my wooden figures, my notebooks, my writing, and my pain. My pain, Señorita Ritter, is my most faithful companion.

Yours,

L.

The spinning-girl retreats and advances
to the hum of the big wheel,

I was in the second last year of high school when the
first of a series of misfortunes occurred. My father worked for
the railway company and was away a lot, and given his frequent
absences from home, it took him a long time to notice what
was happening. I, on the other hand, who lived at home with
Mother, Teresa, and a few other servants, soon realized that
something serious was happening. My mother, who had always
been a strong and even buxom woman, at least from her late
childhood—evident from the family photographs hanging in
the hallway—began to lose weight noticeably. Once a week,
while I sat in the living room polishing my collection of wooden
figures at the coffee table or reading a book in the armchair by
the window, Teresa would sit at the sewing machine that was set
up in the corner, altering clothes with the skill of a seamstress.
On more than one occasion, I was shooed out of my domain by
the two women—I would have to interrupt my reading or leave
off arranging the wooden figures halfway through—so that my
mother could try on one of the garment's Teresa was altering
for her. Through the frosted glass doors of the living room, I
could see their blurry silhouettes engaged in what looked like a
dance: Mother would have her arms raised above her head and
Teresa would be bent forward, adjusting the waist of her dress
and pinning the hem and the cleavage with pins pressed between

her lips and seemingly stuck to her tongue. Through the glass doors, I could hear them whispering and laughing to each other. But the pins never seemed to drop from Teresa's mouth. When they finished, Mother would come out smiling and bustling, sometimes humming, or giving Teresa one final instruction: "Don't go to too much trouble" or "I need it for tomorrow." When I returned to the living room, Teresa would already be happily engaged in her sewing. The satisfaction she got from pleasing her employer was apparent in the way she puffed out her chest and squared her shoulders. Loose multicolored threads from all the unpicking and re-sewing would remain strewn all over the carpet for days, and would eventually blend into the fibers after a few days of us trampling over them.

Teresa took care of Mother as if she were a child: she brushed her hair in the mornings and gave her a manicure every Monday (to this day I still remember the pungent smell of the red nail polish). Even so, Mother began to take on a glum appearance. She tried to hide the lines on her thin and worn face with foundation, over which she would then apply some blush and red lipstick. But the makeup just highlighted her deep eye sockets and the dark circles under them. The thick cord-like veins standing out on her hands and the tufts of gray hair sprouting on her head gave her a Medusa-like appearance. Her secret visits into town became more frequent. I dropped enough hints that I was worried about her health and tried broaching the subject with her over dinner several times, hoping she would reassure me she was feeling all right. But her general state of nervousness rendered her oblivious to my overtures and she avoided the subject completely while serving dinner or drinking her tea.

One night I heard her crying. I went into her bedroom and lay down on the bed beside her and put my head in her lap.

She stroked my hair, as she used to do when I was a child, and said between sobs, "Don't say anything to your father. I'll be all right. The doctor has arranged for Don Gastón to treat me at home. I'll get better."

The mention of treatment was terrifying. I was tormented by the thought of Mother having some sort of terminal illness. I could not sleep at night and imagined the worst: the day of her death, the funeral, the burial. I imagined Señorita Ritter by my side the whole time, holding my hand while I wept disconsolately over my mother's cold body, over her coffin, over her grave. My anxiety was then greatly exacerbated when I thought of living alone in the house with Teresa. I visualized Father sitting on the edge of my bed one morning, kissing my forehead and saying, "Goodbye." I watched him close the door behind him and heard his footsteps fade away as he went down the stairs. I knew deep down he wouldn't want to come back, or indeed have any reason to come back. I would become bitter and be hopelessly alone.

Within a few days, Mother had made all the necessary arrangements to follow her doctor's orders. Father would go away for work on Mondays and Mother would receive treatment on Tuesdays. And this is how, after a couple of years without seeing Don Gastón, fate brought us together again, this time, though, in rather unfortunate circumstances. We would have tea together in the living room, which Teresa served to us in the silver tea set, and we would discuss the latest things we had been reading. We rarely exchanged books. And we never mentioned the library. In a way, we both avoided bringing up the past. There was some kind of underlying awkwardness that neither of us dared speak of.

At 2:00 p.m. sharp, Teresa would appear at the doorway in the living room. Don Gastón would pick up his medical bag, excuse himself, and follow Teresa upstairs to Mother's bedroom, where she was waiting for him. They would be locked away up there for exactly one hour, which seemed an interminable length of time to me. I waited for him outside on the balcony, to make sure he didn't leave without giving me his weekly medical report. I would sit in the rocking chair, carving wooden figures with the sharp ivory-handled knives, rocking to the rhythm of Teresa's soft songs that the breeze carried over from the kitchen, where she was preparing dinner or baking a cake. I had been working on the reproduction of Señorita Ritter—the missing librarian in my collection—for a long time. But I was never satisfied with my results and every Tuesday I would start all over again. On Sundays I would send the gardener out to cut some wood from the same trees the rest of the figures came from. Trying to capture her form in the best piece of willow wood was my favorite pastime, and a productive way to distract myself while waiting for Don Gastón to finish doing what he needed to do.

At 3:00 p.m. sharp, he would emerge in the same way each time: with bright but aloof eyes and pencil thin mustache above pursed lips, muttering a few words indicating a possible improvement that would never come to pass, and then bidding me a stiff farewell. Mother would lock herself in her room for the rest of the afternoon. Teresa would take her in some tea just before nightfall, and then, when I went to bed, I would hear her crying quietly from my room next door.

Why are you crying, Mother? Why are you crying?

*The one-year wife is recovering and happy,
a week ago she bore her first child,*

I'M HERE, MAMÁ.

On the other side of this wall, listening to you crying, waiting patiently for you to call me to your half-empty bed and hug me tenderly. You can keep crying, Mamá. And if you'll allow me, I'll cry with you too. I'll cry the desolate tears of an orphan, because the moment we cling tight to each other, you will shrink from my arms and become one with this pain that fills my insides, my muscles, and my brain. Shared, our grief is dignified; alone and separated by this damned wall, it is just unbecoming.

Rock me in your arms like you did when I was little, Mamá. Let me occupy a place close to your heart. Share with me the love and sense of wonder of childbirth, not its agonizing pain. Tell me that everything is going to be all right, that you will smile as I fall serenely asleep with your fingers knotted in my hair. I want to dream of cotton candy and perpetual summer days, Mamá. Stay with me the whole night, guardian of my dreams. Don't leave me alone with the demons that haunt me in my recurring nightmares.

I'm here, Mamá. Can't you see me anymore? Or are you just a ghost that inhabits the room next door and occasionally occupies a place at the table. Maybe you've gone away with Father on a train.

I'm here, Mamá. You've forgotten how to be with me.

L.

*The jour printer with gray head
and gaunt jaws works at his case . . .
his eyes get blurred with the manuscript,*

I DON'T KNOW WHAT DAY IT IS TODAY.

This morning the woman with purple hair got into the shower stall with me and said she wouldn't leave until she made sure I washed properly. There was no way I was going to shower in the presence of a woman. I tried opening the door to go back to my room but she went to block me and I hit her on the nose accidentally with my elbow and gave her a nosebleed. The nurse showed up in the blink of an eye. He restrained me and dragged me down the corridor. The floor alarm kept blaring and there was total chaos. When the situation was deemed to be under control—in other words, when I was subdued—and once the nurse had stopped the nosebleed by packing the nose with gauze, in a muffled voice the woman with purple hair began to explain that I hadn't actually attacked her.

"Did you hit her?"

"No."

"But she was bleeding."

"It was an accident."

"So then you did hit her."

"Well yes, I hit her, but without meaning to. She got in front of me just as—"

"Why did you hit her?"

"I already told you I didn't mean to hit her!"

This and other similar interrogations were repeated for the rest of the morning to evaluate if I hadn't, in fact, lashed out in unprovoked violence or uncontrollable anger. A gray-bearded man took notes, writing down every word that came out of my mouth without taking his eyes off me, and pointing his chin at me.

The nurse and the police officer stationed by my door escort me to Dr. O'Malley's office. Without a word of greeting, Dr. O'Malley gets up from behind his desk, goes to the door, and asks me to follow him. The police officer and the nurse follow behind us. After walking down corridor after corridor, we cross through the administrative area of the building, until we reach the shower area. I begin to suspect that Dr. O'Malley himself is going to force me to have a shower and I start breathing hard. He makes a weary gesture with his hand to dismiss the bodyguards. Once inside the shower area, he guides me by the shoulders over to the mirror.

It takes me a few seconds to recognize my own image: my hair is long, dark stubble covers my face, and my once solid frame looks rather flabby.

"Take a good look at yourself. Take a close look."

I have long dirty fingernails, acne all over my face, dark circles under my eyes, oily hair, chapped lips, and yellow teeth. I smile at myself—whether out of pity or because I realize such a state is a kind of achievement in itself, I can't say.

When I get back to my room, I notice that the white medical file hanging in the plastic holder on my door has been replaced with a yellow file. I have my lunch (or maybe dinner?). They'll be back soon to take me to the showers again.

*The fare-collector goes through the train—
he gives notice by the jingling
of loose change,*

Weeks went by with no change, until in the end Father finally noticed something wasn't right with Mother. I know this because one Sunday after dinner I heard them arguing in their room. I couldn't understand what they were saying, but I could guess what it was about. On Monday morning, before he left for work, Father sat down on the edge of my bed and pulled the sheet from my head. "Keep an eye on your mother, Son. Don't let her out of your sight," he said with a serious expression on his face, the same expression he had that time when he caught me red-handed with one of the wooden figures under the sheets. Mother didn't come down for breakfast and I kept guard outside her room. Finally, around midmorning, she emerged from her room. She didn't expect to find me sitting there with a book between my knees and she almost spilled the already cold cup of tea she was carrying in her hands. I got up and begged her to tell me what was going on. But she just went downstairs and started giving Teresa orders at the top of her voice.

"Let me at least come with you into town."

"Everything's fine, darling. You don't have to worry about me."

"Mother—"

"Don't push it, dear, please."

She wouldn't look at me anymore, not even to give me an occasional glance.

Father was away for several weeks after the argument with Mother, but even so, he made sure to phone home a few times each week and he would ask to speak to me. I would tell him about school and what I was reading. He would babble something about his work ("new routes to cover" . . . "very busy" . . . "the company is expanding"). Finally, he would ask me about Mother in a dry and, to my mind, slightly anxious voice. I was too ashamed to tell him what I really thought. After a moment of silence, we would then say goodbye and hang up.

Years ago, back when Father first started working for the railway company, he would sit on the porch in the evenings and read the newspaper. Imitating him, I would pick up a magazine or brochure lying around the house and pretend I was reading too. Sometimes we would take walks together around the property, and on a couple of occasions, I accompanied him into town to run his errands. He would introduce me to everyone as his son and people would smile at me and be friendlier than usual. Father was a nice person. My best memory from those days was the summer when just the two of us went to the beach for the weekend (Mother doesn't like the sea). Father came home on the Friday, and over dinner he said, "Pack your things, Son. We're going to the beach tomorrow." He continued cutting his steak calmly, with his white napkin tucked into his shirt collar and spread over his clean and starched uniform. His calm demeanor made what seemed to me like a bold and spontaneous decision sound as though the trip had been arranged in advance. "It's a men's getaway. Just you and me." I turned to Mother, seeking her approval. She took a sip of her drink with pursed lips and didn't look at either of us.

We got up just before dawn the next morning, and to my great surprise, Father let me drive his car to the train station. This alone would have made the trip worthwhile. Before he handed me the keys, I noticed he made sure Mother was still asleep. In a firm but patient voice, he told me what I needed to do: "Slow down. Change gear. Step on the clutch, step on the clutch! Turn on the blinkers. All right, turn them on again. Check the rearview mirror. Here we are. Stop the car. Park here, in reverse." It was the first and only time I had driven a car. Father said I did very well and I believed him. It was strange to see Father at the railway station without his smart gray uniform with a Mao collar, stripes around the cuffs and down the shoulders, and a line of gold buttons that ran down his chest; and without his rather fetching railway cap. Some nights I would secretly try the cap on. It fell down over my eyes and the brim rested on the bridge of my nose, while its smell—a mixture of cologne, sweat, and tobacco— permeated my nostrils.

It was already light when we boarded the train. Father took out the newspaper from his leather briefcase and, taking his lead, I took out my book. But because of the excitement of the trip, coupled with the fact that I was sitting next to my father and had his full attention—or at least I was his sole companion—no matter how hard I tried to focus on the story, my mind kept wandering. I read the same page over and over again until the landscape through the train window gradually became wilder. Father rested the newspaper on his knee, his index finger marking the page he'd been reading. He seemed lost in thought, while admiring the changing colors of the vast countryside speeding by. I followed his lead again, and surrendered my gaze to the scenery whirling past. As the miles sped by, the expression on Father's face gradually softened and his body seemed to relax to the rhythmic rocking of the train carriage. So much so that his newspaper slipped to the floor without his noticing it. We arrived at the station nearest to the coast and one could say that Father looked happy when he got off the train. It was now only a short bus ride to our destination and I was amazed to hear him whistling all the way there.

We ate whatever we felt like—ice cream, fries, hamburgers, triple decker tuna sandwiches—we played racquetball on the shore, and we swam together. When the sun was at its peak and the heat was unbearable, he gave me a drink of his ice-cold beer. "Don't tell your mother. It's secret men's business and it stays between us." At night we played dominoes against two old men who were staying at our small hotel, a colonial house with wide verandas that was very close to the shore. Father was in a good mood and laughed not only when we won a hand, but also when we lost. My father from the beach was a happy and cheerful man. I'm not sure if I was happy at the time, but I know that at least I felt good.

Father and I shared a large and comfortable double room. It had its own kitchen, but we didn't use it, not even to make ourselves a cup of coffee. I woke up in the middle of the night, disoriented, to what sounded like a party winding up in the distance. Father's bed was empty and the worst thoughts went through my head. I peeked into the bathroom but it was empty. Where could he have gone at this hour? I walked barefoot down the verandas that encircled the central courtyard of the house. The cheeky sounds of the crickets only increased my despair. The front door was locked so I ran back to the room to get the keys the landlord had given us. When I got back to the room,

I noticed the lace curtains fluttering on the windows, and this reminded me there was a private balcony in the room. I walked gingerly toward the curtains, the fear caught in my throat. In the moonlight, I saw Father leaning against the railing that overlooked the street behind the hotel. He was singing softly and out of time to the song fading in the distance. He was swaying lightly, dancing with himself, imitating the expressive gestures of the singer, and giving himself fully to the phantom crowd. When the piece finished, he stirred the water from the melted ice cubes in his glass, the same glass in which the ice had clinked throughout our game of dominoes. I was relieved to know that Father was still there with me and, to all appearances, he seemed happy. I went back to bed. He crawled into his side of the bed a little while later and I watched him until his deep breathing lulled me to sleep.

On the bus ride back to the station to take the train home, Father looked tanned and happy. Maybe it was the golden countryside whizzing by through the train window, or the feeling of regret that the weekend was over, or the changing expressions on Father's face, or else just a premonition, but all the way home I felt an uneasiness in my chest. As we got closer to our destination, Father started shifting uneasily in his seat and the expression on his face would sometimes freeze. His shoulders stiffened and the sparkle in his eyes faded. By the time we reached our town, Father had gone back to his old self.

He drove the car in a silence that hardened as we approached our house. At the same time, my unease became unbearable. A knot tightened in my chest and rose to my throat. This feeling soon turned into one of guilt—the guilt associated with having done something wrong. Guilt turned into fear, and my heart started pounding furiously. I could feel the pounding in my temples, the veins popping on my neck and even on my eyelids, as we set our suitcases down at the front door and put the key in the lock to open it. I heard sounds in the kitchen. Instinctively, I made to go to the living room to try to dispel my uneasiness by seeking the company of my books and the wooden figures. But just at that moment Mother came out to greet us and—like a slap to the face—our discomfort assumed physical form.

That night, feeling utterly tormented, I could not stop vomiting. Teresa ran back and forth between the kitchen and my bedroom with various broths and infusions to try to settle my upset stomach, while Mother just stood by watching me from the corner of my room with an almost stern expression. Illness was my punishment and I deserved it. Between the retching and the sobbing, I begged Mother to forgive me for having eaten forbidden foods and for having drunk beer. For things that had nothing to do with the darkness inside me, that itself was eating away at me.

To my surprise, Mother didn't scold or punish me. She even stayed with me until I got well. The next morning I felt deep shame over breaking down and betraying my father's trust; for having let him down in some way (although I never confessed to Mother how happy he was, how happy we were, without her). But Father didn't seem bothered by my treachery either. Everything at home went back to the way it was before. However, I for one made it a point never to disappoint my father again.

P.M.

The following week Father left without saying goodbye to me at bedtime. I heard his footsteps fade down the stairs and the front door close behind him. I had a fearful premonition I would never see him again. In despair, I put on a robe and ran out after him. I was too late. He had already left in his car to go to the station. I tore down the sidewalks and the main street, hoping to catch up with him before the train left. I jumped several fences and took a shortcut until I reached the station. I could still see the smoke from the locomotive. The ticket collector blocked my path. I told him the train driver was my father and that I had something very important I had to tell him, but he didn't believe me and he wouldn't give in to my pleas to let me get through. A whistle announced the departure of the train and that's when I lost my temper. I threw myself over the barrier separating us, and in the tussle between the two of us, his bag of coins spilled all over the ground. I took advantage of the situation to sneak between his legs. I ran through the turnstile and raced to the platform just as the train left. I ran along the train tracks until I could no longer see the train. When I could bear it no longer, I cried out: "Forgive me, Father!"

The drover watches his drove,
he sings out to them that would stray,

FATHER,

Don Gastón's visits don't seem to be helping Mother. What's more, she goes into town frequently and refuses my offer to accompany her. She's gone for what seems like an eternity. And when she comes back home, she looks exhausted and withered. She rarely comes down for dinner. At night, from my bedroom, I can hear her crying in her room. I want to go to her, to ask her what's wrong, to lie down next to her and hug her, but I know it would not be an opportune time. It almost never is. Her pain seeps through the wall, through the door into my room, like poisonous gas. I'm afraid she will leave us. I'm afraid you will leave us. Come back soon, Father.

L.

The torches shine in the dark that hangs
on the Chattahoochee or Altamahaw;

I WROTE AND THEN burned that note by the lake. I read
somewhere that it can help you to feel better if you write down your
feelings and then release them symbolically by burning the paper.
Days, weeks, months went by, but I didn't notice any improvement.
Maybe because there wasn't enough room on that bit of paper—
nothing more than ashes now—to write down what I really feel. Or
because I can't stand the thought of letting my father down . . . again.

*The Wolverine sets traps on the creek
that helps fill the Huron,*

A.M.

Things haven't been going well since the incident in the showers. The nurse, previously only in charge of giving me my medicines and escorting me from one part of the building to another, now accompanies the woman with purple hair to watch me at meal times. As if that weren't enough, it's been decided that I must go down to the dining room to have my meals, where the nurse and the woman with purple hair sit one on either side of me, and where I have to share the table with strangers.

When I enter the dining room for breakfast or lunch (I'm already asleep by dinnertime), there's a momentary silence and all eyes converge on me. After that, everyone goes back to what they were doing, but making sure they can still see me. Many of them greet the nurse; some even shake his hand and call him by his name. When they go up to him, I avoid looking at them. They give off bad vibes.

The people in here are weird. For instance, there's the man with the mustache who's been eating at our table for the past few days. I've noticed he waits for me to arrive so he can sit down opposite me. He doesn't take his eyes off me while eating, the soup dripping down his chin or the puree staining his overalls when he misses his mouth or when he's not paying attention to what he's doing. There's also the girl with braided hair. She has come up to me a few times just to stare at me. As soon as I finish my plate, she stands up in a dramatic, almost theatrical way, and walks off without looking back. What is more suspicious is that even the staff act strangely. When I first started going down to the dining room to eat, various people would serve me at the buffet. Now the only one who serves me is the fat woman with the apron that says "Lucy". I've tried cutting in line in front of the nurse or letting the woman with purple hair go before me, but somehow it's always Lucy that ends up serving me.

I need to feel secure again. That's why I told the woman with purple hair I wanted to have my breakfast and lunch in my room, like I did before. She just gave me a look and rolled her eyes. She's the one who probably arranged for me to have my meals in the dining room because she's afraid that if we're alone in my room together I might attack her again. She wants revenge. She's an idiot!

P.M.

I spoke with the nurse. I told him I knew what the woman with purple hair was trying to do. I asked him to tell her she has nothing to fear from me, that I don't want to hurt her. I'm not going to attack her. Why would I do that? I'm not a brute.

"Please ask them to let me have my meals in my room again."

"Listen, Bruce Lee, she's not the one who decides. You need to ask Dr. O'Malley." I could hear a note of complicity with the woman with purple hair in the tone of his voice.

"When do I get to see the doctor again?"

"In a month, maybe . . ."

He must be joking. Expose me to this group of crazies for another thirty days? I have to find a way to bring my appointment forward as soon as possible. It's crucial that Dr. O'Malley knows and understands my well-being is at stake.

In walls of adobie, in canvas tents, rest hunters and trappers after their day's sport.

"WHY DO YOU want to eat in your room?"

"For the sake of my well-being, Doctor."

"Why do you say that?"

"I just know they're up to something."

"Who's up to something?"

"Everyone, Doctor. They spy on me, they watch me closely while I eat, and that woman . . . Lucy. I don't like her."

"You have nothing to fear. No one is planning anything against you, and if anyone tries anything, you're well protected."

"By who?"

"By the carers, Susana, David . . ."

"What if they're in on it?"

"I can assure you they're not."

"Doctor, please . . ."

"Are you still writing in your notebook?"

I nodded.

"What are you writing about?"

I stayed silent.

"Don't you want to tell me?"

I remained silent.

"That's fine. You don't have to tell me."

I took him at his word and didn't answer.

"It's good that you're writing. You could write down your fears. That would help to release them."

"They're not just fears, Doctor."

"Do you draw?"

"No."

"Would you like to try out something?"

I didn't answer.

"Let's try this: write down your fears every morning and then next to them write down what would help you to overcome them. What would make you feel better."

"I don't usually know what would make me feel better or

how to overcome my fears.”

“Then for every fear, write down two good things or two positives about yourself, about your life.”

“What if I don’t have anything positive to say?”

“Don’t you think there’s anything positive about yourself?”

“I don’t know . . .”

“Try hard. Think of something good about yourself.”

“But what if I can’t think of anything good?”

“We all have something good about ourselves. For example, they say I do a good barbecue.”

“I read books. But reading may not be such a good thing . . .”

“Why would reading not be a good thing?”

“I don’t know. No one’s ever said it to me.”

“Do you need someone to tell you what things are good or not?”

“I guess so.”

“And if no one says anything to you about yourself . . .”

“Then I assume there’s nothing good about me.”

“Why?”

"Well, because no one said anything good about me."

"It's good that you read. That's a positive thing."

"So that would be an affirmation that reading is a good thing then, wouldn't it?"

"Yes. That might work. Let's see, how would you write down your affirmation?"

"I like to read."

"That's fine. Do you know why it's a good thing?"

"No."

"Because it's something real. It's something real and positive about you."

"How do I know it's real?"

"Do you like to read?"

"Yes."

"Then it's real."

"What if I don't want to write about any good things?"

"Then don't. Do it when you're ready."

"No. I mean if I want to write about bad things."

"Do you want to write about bad things?"

"Maybe."

"Bad things about what?"

"About me."

"What do you want to write?"

"I don't know."

"Do you think there are bad things about you?"

"Yes."

"Why?"

"Ha!"

"Why do you think there are bad things about you?"

"Because I'm in here."

"Does that make you a bad person?"

"I guess so."

"You're not a bad person. You have a mental condition."

"A condition that makes me a bad person."

"Not necessarily."

"You don't think I'm bad?"

"No. You're not bad."

"Then why am I locked up in here and being watched all the time?"

"Because you need help. But you'll get better. You want to get better, don't you?"

"How will I get better?"

"You'll get better with the help we're providing you."

"How can you be so sure there are good things about me? Tell me!"

"We all have good things about ourselves."

"I don't!"

"You like to read. That's a good thing."

"Doctor, please!"

"It's true. It's a good thing and I'm telling you that. Accept it."

"You know what I did, Doctor."

"People make mistakes. It doesn't mean that—"

"Oh go to hell, Dr. O'Malley! Go to hell!"

It was almost night when I left the office in a wheelchair. The nurse adroitly wheeled me down the corridors, whistling a familiar tune I couldn't place. The bright white lights of the elevator, the freezing cold corridors, the squeaking of the wheels, the smell of bleach, they all seemed new, shocking, out of place. When we got back to the room, the nurse helped settle me into bed. He lifted me effortlessly out of the wheelchair, placed me on the bed, bandaged my knuckles, and tucked me in tight. He stayed with me for a while. I heard him scribbling things down on a piece of paper, arranging vials, adjusting the height of the bed. Then he went over to the door and swapped the yellow file in the plastic holder for a red one, before leaving and closing the door behind him. The darkness swallowed me up whole.

*The living sleep for their time . . .
the dead sleep for their time,*

AS I MAKE my way along the track, my feet kick up small clouds of dust while stones get stuck in the soles of my boots. The house is five hundred feet from the main road. It's a warm and humid morning and I walk along under the shade of the trees. I stop at the front gate and lift the mailbox lid. It was never locked. "There's nothing in here," its hollow cavity echoes back at me. The latch on the gate, as always, is stuck. But it offers no resistance when I use my old trick to open it.

I go up the paved path leading to the front of the house. I feel the cool shade of the dozens of old trees planted on either side. The imposing façade of the house still reflects the prosperity of years past. Its design takes the shape of a bird in flight: a central nave and two wings spread wide open on each side. The front porch is wide and cool, and is furnished with rocking chairs and comfortable armchairs. The sparse décor is made up of natural materials: plants, tree stumps, and objects made of stone or wood.

I enter the house and am greeted by familiar faces hanging on the wall. This image takes me back to the time when I went to the library and located the genealogical records of each of the people in the portraits in the hall. I walk along the corridors without haste, noticing the details that in the past went unnoticed in the day-to-day routine of living: the wallpaper peeled at the edges; worn skirting boards; crooked lamps. A musty odor and the smell of resin and wet newspapers permeate every corner. As I approach the kitchen, the odors mix with an oily smell, and there is a sticky, greasy coating on the surrounding surfaces.

I reach the living room. There are traces of me everywhere here. I can feel my own presence. My energy hangs suspended in the air like the curtains. It sits on the sofa like an entity. As I walk around the room, a feeling of warmth overcomes me and I begin to feel more and more at home. I sit down on the worn carpet and leaf through a book that has been tossed on the floor. I get distracted for a while reading a few poems, anticipating a line or two out loud, unable to resist the urge to recite the verses from memory. When I finish, I get up and gaze at the high shelf where the wooden figures stand. The entire collection of workers and townspeople greet me warmly with a collective wave. Some make little curtsies that make me smile. Oh how I've missed them! I take down the wood and ivory box, my little treasure chest, and blow the dust off the lid to reveal the engravings on it. The box itself is a work of art. The felt lining inside has crumbled and broken away, and the miniature accessories are covered in a fine red dust.

I carefully match each of the accessories with the corresponding figure, to give them a specific purpose, to contextualize their lives:

The contralto sings,

The carpenter dresses his plank,

The family sits down to dinner together,

The pilot takes the wheel,

The harpooner brandishes his harpoon,

The duck-shooter cleans his rifle,

The priests pray,

The spinning-girl sits at her spinning wheel,

The farmer gazes over his fields,

The madman is locked up (he will never sleep any more as he did in the cot in his mother's bedroom),

The typesetter works at the printing press,

The patient lies on the operating table,

A young girl is sold at auction,

The machinist expertly uses his tools,

The policeman makes his rounds,

The bored watchman marks those who pass by,

A young man drives the train (I love him though I do not know him),

The half-breed straps on his light boots to compete in the race,

The youths holding a turkey shoot lean on their rifles,

The groups of newly arrived immigrants gather on the lakeshore,

The cane cutters raise their sickles,

The overseer gallops on his horse,

The musicians play the trumpet and the dancers dance,

A youth lies awake in bed listening to the rain,

The hunter sets a trap,

The Indian street vendor offers her goods for sale,

The art collector admires a painting,

The sailor throws out the anchor,

Two sisters sit weaving together,

The one-year wife cradles her newborn in her arms,

The woman sews at the mill,

The workman bangs his hammer,

The clerk takes notes,

The sign painter paints a billboard,

A boy runs along the train tracks,

The bookkeeper goes over the accounts,

The fastidious shoemaker shines shoes,

The conductor waves the baton vigorously,

The orchestra takes its cues from the conductor,

A child is baptized,

The captain of the boat on the lake gazes at the horizon,

The herdsman guides his herd with whistles,

The peddler sweats with his pack on his back; people haggle with him,

The bride waits dressed in her white dress,

A vagrant stands stupefied by opium on the sidewalk,

The prostitute is dressed in tacky garb,

The President, with a sash around his chest, is surrounded by cabinet ministers,

Three old matrons stand gossiping in the square,

The fishermen store their catch,

A plainsman crosses the plain,

The fare collector opens his bag to collect the fares,

The tiler lays the floor, the carpenter repairs the roof, the bricklayers mix the mortar,

The farmer sows seeds with hope,

The woodsman chops a log with his axe,

The hunters and trappers camouflage themselves in the forest,

An old married couple sleeps in bed together.

All my figures are a part of me.

"And such as it is to be of these more or less I am." (Walt Whitman, "Song of Myself")

Something wet comes up around my boots; a sticky puddle slowly floods the room. The liquid is warm and bubbly. The stream trickles sprightly and gently, swirling between my feet. Where is it coming from? I follow its trail, coming in through the doorway. It has spread throughout the corridors, flowing down from the staircase. Thirteen lifeless bodies lie floating in a purplish puddle on the bottom marble step.

Climax

From guttural to piercing
a cry escapes

rigid, but alive
arms and legs, quiver

neck and spine,
shame and guilt, retract

the chalice of red wine
that intoxicates and liberates, flows

afterwards, spent, everything becomes
heavy, languid, it fades away
                          or loses importance.

There were two orgasms.

L.

*The lunatic is carried at last to
the asylum a confirmed case,*

*He will never sleep any more as he did
in the cot in his mother's bedroom;*

THAT TUESDAY Don Gastón arrived at the usual time and Teresa led him into the living room. He found me sitting with my entire collection spread out on the coffee table. I was using a magnifying glass to compare the details of the original figures with the new one I had made of Señorita Ritter. Intrigued, he took the opportunity to look over the group of wooden figures. He leaned forward with his hands clasped behind his back and his eyes darted from one to the other. I took advantage of his interest to ask his opinion.

"These are the figures from the original collection carved by my grandfather and his father, and this is the one I carved," I said, showing him Señorita Ritter. "I used wood from the same willow tree and the same carving knives that my ancestors used. I used the same carving technique as them. What do you think of the result?"

Don Gastón said nothing. He just ripped the figure from my hands and began studying it intently. His fingertips turned white from the pressure of his grip. He slid his fat fingers over the torso, down to the skirt, and intermittently ran them over the slope of the small nose I had sculpted into the face that lacked features. I noticed a hint of recognition in his eyes, an unusual glow, as he ran his fingers over her. I interrupted him to ask him to pick up a random figure and compare it with mine. He walked around the table, rubbing at Señorita Ritter the whole time. With his left hand he grabbed at a sly-looking figure in the corner, standing right next to the train driver. The figure he picked up was wearing a white coat and black pants, but showed no other signs of his trade. "A pharmacist," Don Gastón said, with a smile that stretched his mustache. Teresa poked her head in through the doorway at that moment. With a haughty gesture, he placed both effigies in the palm of my hand.

"They lack distinctive facial features," he said, without looking at me.

He picked up his medical bag and walked off behind Teresa. I stood there for a few minutes, staring at the figure of the supposed pharmacist in my hand, rubbing my thumb over his rough straight cuts. Don Gastón was right, it lacked distinctive features. It was so flat that it blended in with all the others, just like the figure standing with his feet together and arms at his sides and his right hand pointed like a blade. I looked around for it and spotted him among the group. I placed the three figures in question on the window sill, bathed in natural light, and inspected each one under a magnifying glass. I ran my fingers over them with curiosity, with pleasure, with rage. I placed them side by side: the pharmacist, the librarian, and the young man with the hand pointed like a blade.

It all made sense.

In the kitchen, Teresa was singing an old song by the stove; the same one as always. I approached her from behind, walking in step to the rhythm of the tune. When she finished the verse, I put an end to her song with a clean cut to her throat. The silver cup she was holding dropped from her hand and bounced on the floor where it made a ping sound. I stole quietly out of the kitchen, somewhat dazed by the accelerated thumping of my own heartbeat. With my sweaty hands stuffed in my pants pockets, I went up the stairs and put my ear to the door of the master bedroom. The sound of my mother's gasps electrified me, made my mouth go dry, made my lips go numb. I squeezed the three figures in my left pocket and the ivory-handled knife in my right pocket tightly. I nudged the door open gently with my shoulder. Through the crack in the open doorway, the sight of my mother lying under the canopy while Don Gastón stood on the floor at the edge of the bed—next to his still closed medical bag and with his black pants down around his ankles—thrusting vigorously into her, stunned my senses. His plump fingers were white from the pressure of his grip on Mother's ankles that were fluttering over her head like flags in the wind. "Keep an eye on your mother, Son. Don't let her out of your sight."

Inertia is both a reflex as well as a state of mind.

I made the first cut across his back. And this would have sufficed, but I carved his body with multiple stabs. His warm, oily bodily fluids soaked my hands, splattered my clothes and my face. I turned him over and sat on his chest, pinning his already lifeless body down. I wanted to erase the features from his face, but my hysterical mother stopped me. She pushed me off him as best she could. I cut her too. I cut her without meaning to. Although, in my place, Father would have ripped her to shreds if he had known. Or if he finds out one day.

I suppose that when Mother fled from the room she went to seek help. I lost track of time. All I remember is the moment when people began to appear—first some of the neighbors, then the police—and I tried to explain to them, but no one seemed to understand; they just stared at me in horror as I repeated, "They were made of wood. They were made of wood."

The malformed limbs are tied to the anatomist's table,

MY VISIT WITH Dr. O'Malley complicated matters. At my last session with him, I wore myself out trying to explain why I should be allowed to go back to eating in my room. It was obvious that the others were planning a very dangerous conspiracy, and that they were in league with the dining room staff. I was afraid they would sneak into my room at night and steal my few belongings—my notebook, my pen, my figures, my books, or even worse—kill me.

The mood between the nurse and the woman with purple hair and me turned sour on the trips to the dining room, especially when I stopped eating. It wasn't rebellion on my part so much as a safety measure: I didn't trust Lucy. What if she were slowly poisoning my food? After a few days of me going on hunger strike, the nurse stayed with me from breakfast to lunch; together we watched the dining room fill up, empty out, and fill up again. By the end of the afternoon, everyone had gone and we were the only ones left there. The plates with breakfast (scrambled eggs and toast) and lunch (roasted chicken thigh fillet, white rice, and a boring salad) sat uneaten before me. The wall clock showed it was almost 6:00 p.m. The nurse rose from the bench and pulled me roughly to my feet. His usual mocking smile was gone, replaced by a strained expression, jaw tight, eyes narrowed. He dragged me toward the exit. I tripped over whatever lay in my path. His grip on my arm was fierce. I struggled to release myself

from his iron grip, but he was too strong. I was like a rag doll in
his powerful hand. "You're hurting me," I said. "You're hurting
me!" I repeated. I whirled my head around, looking in vain for
someone to help me, and that's when I realized with horror what
was happening: they were carrying out their macabre plan. I was
in the grip of the strongest and most brutal of the group, with no
one else around to witness it, and I was weak with hunger. But
strength would not help me anyway; I was no match for him.
Nor would luck be on my side in a momentary stand against my
opponent. What I needed to do was conserve my energy in order
to confuse the nurse, to outsmart him so I could escape. Despite
the struggle, he managed to maintain his grip on some part of my
body—my arm, my wrist, my ankle . . . his fingers grabbed at my
throat and that's when my survival instinct kicked in. I dropped
to the floor in a pretend faint, curling instinctively into the fetal
position. The nurse bore down on me in triumph in his final
attempt to overpower me.

Inertia is both a reflex as well as a state of mind.

The moment his warm flesh came into contact with mine,
I pulled the pen out of my pocket and stabbed him with it in
the neck. I felt his limbs twitch involuntarily, like a wounded
cockroach. I rolled him off me and made for the exit as quickly
as my shaky legs would allow. I peered down the corridor. His
accomplices were already lying in wait, ready to fight the final
battle.

The city sleeps and the country sleeps,

FOG SITS OVER the lake, bright gray blue at the bottom edges and blurring with the white clouds higher up. I keep losing sight of the horizon, water and sky blending seamlessly. When I think I can finally see it again, the fog's slow movement gets its way and blots the horizon once more. A boat is bobbing gently in the water, in step with the wind, the closed currents, and the rhythm of my breathing. The boat has an upper and a lower deck and is made of timber. It has white slat railings and an attractive flat roof. It's the most beautiful boat I have ever seen, with small yellow lights and nautical wheels decorating the hull.

Occasional splinters of sunlight pierce through a cloud, but are then swallowed up by the slow-moving fog. It's like watching grass grow. The clear view I have of the lone boat comforts me, provides me company, and gives me a sense of peace. The fog never obscures it. Sudden heavy rain forms a wide curtain of water and the boat vanishes from sight. The rain pummels the lake and drives away the fog. Behind the watery curtain, I picture the boat being lashed by rain, water flooding the deck and the interior, flowing through the maze of cabins, sweeping everything in its path, damaging the wood. Flashes of lightning provide me with momentary glimpses of where I think the boat is, but the lake is as big as an ocean, with no visible borders in sight.

When calm returns after the storm, I gaze at the beauty of the boat's timber frame. It is once more bobbing gently in the placid water. A prism of light appears, cascading over the lake's surface, before disappearing.

I open my eyes for the briefest of moments. I would like to go back to the lake, but there are people giving me medicine to forcibly put me to sleep.

And these one and all tend inward to me,
and I tend outward to them,

And such as it is to be of these
more or less I am,

And of these one and all I weave
the song of myself.

MY PARENTS VISIT me every second Saturday. They hardly say a word to me. They don't listen to me or touch me. They just sit there keeping me company, looking miserable, watching me lying in bed and listening to the sound of the rain beating against my window. Dr. O'Malley talks to them as if I can't understand or as if I'm not even there. When he tells them that I'm going to be fine and that I might be able to go home soon, my father looks relieved. He kisses me on the forehead and leaves. My mother is already waiting for him by the door.

I never had the heart to tell Father, and nor will I ever. I guess this is the cross I have to bear for letting him down again.

Señorita Ritter still takes the trouble to visit me and brings me books wrapped in brown paper. As usual, we don't talk, but we don't need to. What needs to be said is there on every page of the books she gives me.

She's here with me now in the room, as I write down these lines in the last pages of my notebook in crayon. I have the feeling she knows what it is that I am completing today. Sitting in the armchair in the corner, she concentrates her gaze sunward, feeling its weight as sundown approaches. She looks out the window with a calm expression on her face, as if she is sitting for a portrait, as if today there is no need for her to rush off at an appointed time. Occasionally she sighs, and in the sound she makes, I can hear her voice, the one she addressed me informally with that day when she gave me the notebook, saying, "Make good use of it."

With complete frankness I say: I don't know if what I have done is right or wrong; I don't know if it will have served any purpose telling you this story. Today, at the end of your visit, I will give you this notebook which I have been writing in, and you can then be the judge and critic of what I have written. As for me, I will keep these figures side by side on the window sill; the oil-based paint repelled the blood and dirt. The remaining one hundred and six figures are waiting patiently for me back home on the high shelf in the living room. And, for all I know, they may be hatching a plan.

AUTHOR'S NOTE

The epigraphs at the beginning of each chapter and the lines quoted on pages 23 and 120 are taken from Section 15 of the poem "Song of Myself" by Walt Whitman that is included in *Leaves of Grass* (1855). They are not presented in the order of the original poem.

MARÍA PÉREZ-TALAVERA (b. 1985 Valencia, Venezuela) is a writer, librarian, and marketing, communications and information science professional. Her debut novel *Eran de Madera* (Figures of Wood) won the VI Foro/taller Sagitario Ediciones Prize for a Short Novel in Panama in 2019. She has written the short story collection *Umbrales líquidos* (Liquid Thresholds) (Foro/taller Sagitario Ediciones, 2015). Her stories, poetry, and essays have been published in various anthologies, magazines, newspapers, and online publications. English translations of her stories have appeared in *Latin American Literature Today* and *Asymptote*. She lives in Vientiane, Laos.

PAUL FILEV translates from Macedonian and Spanish. He has translated the novels *Alma Mahler* by Sasho Dimoski (Dalkey Archive Press, 2018), *Blue Label* by Eduardo Sánchez Rugeles (Turtle Point Press, 2018), *The Sorrow of Miles Franklin beneath Mount Kajmakčalan* by Ivan Čapovski (Cadmus Press, 2020), and *The Lisbon Syndrome* by Eduardo Sánchez Rugeles (Turtle Point Press, 2022), which was named one of *World Literature Today*'s 75 Notable Translations of 2022. He has also translated the anthology *Contemporary Macedonian Fiction* (Dalkey Archive Press, 2019), and the short story collection *My Husband* by Rumena Bužarovska (Dalkey Archive Press, 2019). He lives in Melbourne.

LOS ANGELES

All WHAT BOOKS feature cover art by Los Angeles painter, printmaker, muralist, and theater and performance artist GRONK. A founding member of ASCO, Gronk collaborates with the LA and Santa Fe Operas and the Kronos Quartet. His work is found in the Corcoran, Smithsonian, LACMA, and Riverside Art Museum's Cheech Marin collection.

As a small, independent press, we urge our readers to support independent booksellers. This is easily done on our website by purchasing our books from Bookshop.org.

WHATBOOKSPRESS.COM

2012

*The Mermaid at the Americana
Arms Motel*
A.W. DEANNUNTIS
NOVEL

The Time of Quarantine
KATHARINE HAAKE
NOVEL

Frottage & Even As We Speak
MONA HOUGHTON
NOVELLAS

*West of Eden:
A Life in 21ˢᵗ Century Los Angeles*
CHUCK ROSENTHAL
MAGIC JOURNALISM

2010

Master Siger's Dream
A.W. DEANNUNTIS
NOVEL

Other Countries
RAMÓN GARCÍA
POEMS

A Giant Claw
GRONK
ESSAY BY GAIL WRONSKY
SPANISH TRANSLATION
BY ALICIA PARTNOY
ART

*Coyote O'Donohughe's
History of Texas*
CHUCK ROSENTHAL
NOVEL

So Quick Bright Things
GAIL WRONSKY
BILINGUAL, SPANISH TRANSLATION
BY ALICIA PARTNOY
POEMS

2009

*Bling & Fringe
(The L.A. Poems)*
MOLLY BENDALL &
GAIL WRONSKY
POEMS

April, May, and So On
FRANÇOIS CAMOIN
STORIES

One of Those Russian Novels
KEVIN CANTWELL
POEMS

*The Origin of Stars
& Other Stories*
KATHARINE HAAKE
STORIES

Lizard Dream
KAREN KEVORKIAN
POEMS

*Are We Not There Yet?
Travels in Nepal,
North India, and Bhutan*
CHUCK ROSENTHAL
MAGIC JOURNALISM

LOS ANGELES